Death's Doorstep

STEPHEN H. PROVOST

Dragon Crown Books 2020
All rights reserved.

ISBN-13: 978-1-949971-16-3

Dedication

Dedicated to... disturbing you, valued reader.

Contents

A thing is not necessarily true
because a man dies for it.

Oscar Wilde

DEATH'S DOORSTEP

I have to...

STEPHEN H. PROVOST

tell this story...

STEPHEN H. PROVOST

before it's...

STEPHEN H. PROVOST

too late.

HELP ME!

I'm saying those words now, because I know what she meant when she was saying them.

She was desperate, and she hoped I would hear her. There's no one to hear me now. I know that. But still I have to try, the way someone bangs on the lid of a coffin if he's buried alive, even though he knows no one will hear.

Help me!

Is this what it's like to be in a coma?

I don't know. I've never been in a coma before. Once I had a nightmare, though, where I couldn't wake up. I was trying to blow out the candles on my birthday cake in one breath, and I had to do it because the wish was so important. The wish was her. That she would join me in Stockholm. But I didn't have enough breath. I ran out.

I woke up gasping, lightheaded, like I was having an asthma attack.

It must have sounded bad, because she shook me awake. She was frantic.

"Wake up!" She was nearly shouting. "God, wake up, Allen!"

And finally, I did.

It was her. My wish. She'd already come true, and we'd been together 20 years. So, what was that dream about?

"You stopped breathing!" She said, out of

breath herself from the panic. She was even sweating. She looked really scared, knitting her eyebrows together the way she does when she can't figure out what to do about something important — something she's scared she can't control.

"It's all right, honey," I told her, shedding my own terror because I had to, to comfort her.

I held her.

I wish I could hold her now, but there aren't any birthday candles to blow out. Just darkness, and everything fading, like I'm trying to stay awake, because I know if I don't, I'm gonna die.

But this is worse than death. It's what they call oblivion. Maybe I'm already dead, just like she is. But I have to explain, because death isn't what I thought it was. It isn't what any of us think it is.

Not that anyone will ever hear this, but I have to try.

Help me!

I feel like I'm losing my breath again, like in that dream, but this isn't a dream. Is it?

Calm down, Allen, I tell myself. Slow, steady breaths. Focus. Think back to the beginning. Maybe if I retrace my steps, I can find a way out of this.

Who am I kidding?

But I have to try. Before it all fades away completely. Before *I* fade away completely.

Okay, okay... Here goes...

Molly

It all started with that visit to the doctor's office. Well, actually, before that, when I realized there was something different about Molly.

She wasn't herself.

I'd met her in a philosophy class at Cal State Fullerton. It had nothing to do with my major, physics. I was taking it because I needed a few extra credits to graduate, and I'd always found philosophy a kick.

Molly stood out right away, mainly because she answered most of the prof's questions before anyone could raise their hand. At first, I thought she was trying to show off to get a good grade.

Then I realized it was just because she knew the answers.

She always got them right.

That was what struck me most about her right away. It wasn't her round cheeks, which looked like red apples when she smiled, or the wavy auburn-red hair that fell down past hear shoulders. It wasn't her eyes or her figure. It was her intelligence.

That's what attracted me to her.

Don't laugh.

I know. Guys are supposed to notice a girl's legs or breasts first, and it's not like I *didn't* notice those things. It's just that they were secondary. And they got more secondary the more I got to know her.

Because Molly wasn't just smart about philosophy, she was smart about me. You know how they say couples can finish each other's sentences for them after they're together for a long time? She was doing that almost from the beginning. At first, I was put off by it. I wanted to tell her things myself, and I didn't like feeling so predictable. Transparent. But after a while, it got to be reassuring — like, "Hey, this person really knows me because she thinks I'm worth figuring out."

It was almost love at first sight, but not exactly. When I first felt that reassurance: That's when I knew she was the one.

We almost didn't get there. About a month after we met, I got an offer to work on a project in Stockholm. It was a *very good* offer: I could earn all the credits I needed to graduate over there. Then I could stay on as part of the team. But it meant Molly and I wouldn't be together, because she said she couldn't come with me. She never told me why, but I knew she was serious, and I never tried to convince her otherwise.

I took the offer anyway, but after a couple of days, I started feeling sick. Nauseated. I went to see a doctor — Dr. Larsson, I think it was — and he told me there was nothing wrong with me, and that's when I realized that I was sick because I couldn't be with Molly.

I quit the project and flew home. The nausea went away.

Molly was a couple of years older than I was, but it didn't matter to either one of us. She took me home to meet her parents after I got back from Stockholm, because she said they might as well meet the man she was going to marry.

How had she known I'd already picked out a ring?

She just did. Or at least she sensed it. That was her. She was intuitive, but more with me than with anyone else. We had this weird connection... I guess we still do. Which explains...

I'm getting ahead of myself.

Her parents. Yes, that's where I was. He was an aeronautical engineer, and she was a lawyer. Now I saw where she'd gotten her brains. But she didn't think like them. They were... conventional, I guess is the word for it. They'd jumped through all the right hoops to get where they were.

Molly hadn't. She never graduated from college because she didn't think she needed to. That philosophy class? It was the only college course she'd ever taken, and she was auditing it, not doing it to get a grade or a diploma or anything like that. She just thought it would be fun.

Her parents were impressed that I'd graduated, but they weren't impressed with *me*. They saw what I'd achieved, but they didn't see who I was.

Molly did.

She's the only one who ever did.

Now I wish she hadn't. Or do I? Maybe the 20 years I had with her were worth what's happening now. But in the moment, it doesn't feel like it, because I'm terrified...

Focus!

The crash... Molly was devastated when her parents died in that plane crash a few years after we got married. It was the first flight ever of the Raptor 99 passenger jet, which Molly's dad had designed. He was so proud of that thing. It had been his life's work, and it crashed the first time they flew it.

It was like the Titanic or the Hindenburg.

It went down over the Bermuda Triangle, of all places.

I don't believe in any of that stuff, but Molly was sure it had something to do with her parents dying. I'm not sure why. Molly was weird that way. She was the most logical, rational person I'd ever met. Smart as a whip, you might say — actually, a whole lot smarter, because whips are kind of stupid. But she would come up with these weird ideas out of nowhere, without any evidence at all.

She'd say she knew where Atlantis was, or that a hurricane was forming in the Gulf of Mexico, even though she hadn't seen the news in days.

"Just trust me," she said. "Always trust me. Is

that so much to ask?"

But I couldn't. I never told her I couldn't, but she was asking me to believe stuff that no one in their right mind would have believed. Except her. And she wasn't crazy. It didn't make sense, but a lot of things don't, do they?

No one ever found her parents' bodies, but Molly swore to me she'd heard her mother's voice calling to her, about a minute after the plane went down: She went back and timed it out after they recovered the black box from the bottom of the sea.

That was all they found.

"You're imagining it," I'd say. There was no way she could have heard her mother's voice from thousands of miles away as she was sinking under the ocean.

"No, I wasn't," she'd insist. "I heard her. She was saying, 'Help me!'"

Like I am now.

I tried to reassure her. That voice in her head hit her almost as hard as her parents dying.

Maybe harder.

After that, she felt this incredible, irrational guilt about it.

"I should have gone to her," she'd say. "I should have helped her."

"How could you?" I asked her.

"I could have," she'd say. "I was just too scared. It's all my fault. I could have."

Times like those, I wished I could've understood her the way she understood me. But she said it didn't matter; that she was glad I didn't have to deal with it, because it was almost too much for her.

She was never quite the same after that, but I thought we were living a pretty normal life for years: She worked as a freelance PR consultant, and I got a job teaching physics at Cal Tech. But maybe I was just kidding myself, like her parents were. Maybe I was just looking at the external stuff, while Molly was stuck inside her own head the whole time.

Sometimes, she'd wake up in the middle of

the night, frantic, saying her mother was calling out to her again.

Help me!

I told her it was just a dream, that it would pass. I'd get her a glass of water or warm milk from the kitchen, and she'd sit there reading until she was finally calm enough to go back to sleep.

But it would always happen again.

I thought it would get better as time passed. You know, the whole "time heals all wounds" thing. My younger brother had died in an accident when I was nine, and it had totally freaked me out at the time. He'd fallen out of a tree, cracked his head, and that had been it. It was all so sudden.

If he could die, and he was younger than me, that meant I could die, too, because I was older that he was. For months, I was afraid to go to sleep, and if I saw trees, I'd walk the other way.

I'd never even thought about death before

that, but then I started thinking about it all the time. Whenever my mom or dad left for work, I was scared they wouldn't come back. I started failing in school because I was afraid that everyone who came to the classroom with a message for the teacher was coming to tell me my parents had died.

After a while, though, I shut it all out. My parents always came home, the trees didn't attack me, and I got distracted by the kind of things that distract kids that age. I signed up for Little League; I collected baseball cards and comic books; later on, I discovered girls.

My grades got better, and I stopped thinking about death so much. I still missed my little brother, and it was weird to think about growing up without him, but as I did grow up, I thought about him less and less, until I forgot how he used to bug me, the way little brothers do, and even what his voice had sounded like.

I thought that was normal, but it wasn't for Molly.

For her, time didn't heal anything. It just made things worse. The more time passed since her mother's death, the more upset she seemed by it. The more she woke up in the middle of the night, saying she'd heard her mom's voice — it even happened sometimes in the daytime, too.

She couldn't let go of the guilt, either. She went to a counselor, who told her it was normal to blame yourself for a loved one's death.

She stopped going after the second session. She said the counselor didn't understand what she was trying to say, and that there wasn't anything wrong with her.

I didn't push it, because I didn't want her to feel like I thought there was.

But I did.

Not in a mean way or in passing judgment; I was just worried, and I didn't know how to *tell her* I was worried without making her feel like some sort of freak.

So I didn't say anything more about it.

Until about a year ago. That's when it

became something more than just "one of those things" about someone you love that you just pass off as being quirky.

I came home one day and found her in her home office, staring blankly at the screen. She'd been working on an assignment for one of her clients, and at first, I thought she was just stuck — you know, like she was waiting for an idea to come to her.

She hadn't heard me come in, and I didn't want to startle her, so I said, "Hey, Moll." But she didn't turn around.

"Hey, Moll!" I said again, louder this time, but she still didn't acknowledge me.

I got worried, so I went up behind her and put my hands on her shoulders.

She jumped so much I thought she might fall out of her chair.

"Jesus, Allen! Don't *do* that!" she said.

"Sorry," I told her.

But she was staring at me with a weird look in her eyes, halfway between crazed and...

empty. Like she was somewhere else. Or had been somewhere else and was trying to come back.

"I thought you were Mom," she said, almost whimpering, and fell in to my arms. The whimpers turned to sobs.

"Something's happening," she said. "I don't know what it is."

"Did you hear your mom again?" I asked. She nodded.

I wanted to ask her what she'd said, but I knew the answer. It was always the same.

Help me!

So, I asked something different this time. "Where is she?"

It was the right question, but also the wrong one.

"I don't know!" Molly almost yelled. "That's what's so awful about it."

"Because they never found her body?"

"No." She shook her head wildly from side

to side. "It's not her body. It's *her*. She's somewhere else. Not at the bottom of the ocean. Somewhere... I don't know. I've got to find her. I've got to save her."

I wanted to tell her, "Your mom's been dead for years," but I knew that would only make things worse.

I tried to hug her, but she stepped back and put both hands to her head, grimacing.

"What's wrong?" I said.

"It's this headache," she said. "It won't go away."

Lapses

It turned out she'd been having these headaches for a while. She hadn't told me because she didn't want to worry me.

"How long have you had them?"

"Since Mom and Dad died."

She'd thought they were from spending too much time in front of the PC. Eye strain. She'd try to sleep them off, but then she'd wake up saying she'd heard her mom crying for help again.

She didn't want to go to the doctor, but I insisted.

He said they were probably migraines and gave her a medicine called something-triptan. He told her to keep the lights dimmer, and the computer screen, too, and not to look at it for too long at a time.

None of that helped at all.

Worse, Molly started having more of those "episodes" — that's what she called them — where she seemed to be somewhere else, and I'd startle the hell out of her. She'd start crying, and I'd end up feeling guilty.

But there was even more to it than that.

She started forgetting things.

Not just goofy things like where she put a pen or her glasses or something like that. Not like pouring orange juice on her cereal. Big things. Like where she grew up.

"What was the name of that place again?" she'd ask.

Santa Monica? You mean Santa Monica?

"Yes, that's it." She'd smile. "Thanks, Allen."

That worried me. I might forget things, but

I'd never once forgotten the name of my hometown. Or our cat, Freya.

"Here kitty-kitty!" Molly called one night when she wanted to pet her.

But of course, Freya didn't come. She was probably insulted. She'd come most of the time if you called her by name, but she was definitely *not* "kitty-kitty." Molly had been the one who insisted on always using her name, so she'd get used to it. She'd never called her "kitty-kitty" before.

"You know she won't come when you call her like that," I said.

"Why not?" It seemed like she really didn't know.

"Because that's not her name," I said.

She seemed embarrassed — like when someone thinks they should know something simple, but doesn't want to admit they don't. Like how to fill your gas tank. Or how long you needed to leave a cup of tea in the microwave.

She didn't want to ask, but finally, she did:

"What's her name again?"

"Whose name?"

"The kitty, silly."

"Freya." I frowned. She could not possibly have forgotten Freya's name.

She must be teasing me.

But she wasn't.

"Yes. Freya. Of course," she said. "Thanks, honey."

She kissed me, but there was something weird about that, too. She never called me "honey." She always called me by my name, or some personal nickname she'd chosen for me, like Alley-Oops! or Allen-a-Dale from *Robin Hood* or something silly like that.

I suddenly realized she hadn't used my name in days. Maybe weeks.

"You seem really absent-minded lately," I said. "I'm worried."

"Really? I hadn't noticed."

"You just forgot Freya's name," I said.

"Who?"

"Freya. The cat."

Freya jumped up into her lap. Maybe she was worried, too.

Molly got this pained look on her face, not like physical pain, but the pain of realizing something wasn't right, and she didn't know how to fix it. Molly had always been great at fixing things. I'd relied on her for it, probably too much.

I realized then that I would have to find a way to fix this, if I could.

I didn't know how.

"Those migraine pills aren't working, are they?" I said.

She shook her head, then admitted, "I forgot where I put them."

It didn't matter. We'd have to go back to the doctor again.

She stepped back from me and looked at me with that pained, empty look, like she thought I was a stranger.

I heard her voice say it then.

Help me!

But her lips didn't move. It was her voice, but it was coming from somewhere else.

Spot

I'd seen something like this happen to my grandfather. He'd had Alzheimer's, and he'd slowly forgotten everything, even his children's names and who they were.

My dad — his son — had stopped going to see him because he said it was too painful. He asked me to go instead. Grandpa thought I was a nurse, but it didn't matter to me. It seemed to cheer him up to have *anyone* to talk to.

Part of me was angry at my dad for not going to see him. What could it have hurt? The old man had only so much time left; why not visit him?

Even if Dad couldn't talk about anything or had to repeat himself, at least he could have *been there*.

I remembered thinking that and started telling myself the same thing when Molly started getting worse.

I would be there for her.

Even if she didn't know who I was. I would stay and just be there. Unlike my mom and dad, we'd never had kids, so there was no one to help if I flaked out. I wouldn't have flaked out anyway. I would never have forgiven myself.

But this wasn't Alzheimer's. It couldn't be. Molly was forty-five years old. You didn't get Alzheimer's that young. It wasn't just migraines, either, though. It had to be something worse than that. I didn't even want to think about what it might be. I didn't want to know the answer. But I had to know, or I couldn't deal with it; I couldn't help her.

"What is it, Doc?" I asked him as he entered the room, X-rays in hand. He took them over a wall of translucent glass or plastic that was lit from the back, and he clipped them up there.

He'd ordered them for her after our last visit, a couple of weeks before, and we'd gone to see the X-ray tech right after that. Then we'd gotten a call from the doctor, who'd set up a second set of X-rays for the following week.

It wasn't clear why, and he wouldn't tell us.

"It's just routine," he'd said at the time. "We need to cover all the bases."

It wasn't just routine.

He kept looking down at his clipboard, avoiding my eyes.

"Well?" I said.

Finally, he looked up and said, "It's a tumor, Allen."

"Cancer? In her head?"

"Her brain," he said. "Look here." He pointed to a spot on the X-rays. It didn't look very big, but there was no missing it. "It's in the area of her brain that affects long-term memory."

I was breathing faster. "It's just a spot. Pretty small. That's good, right?"

"Yes, but not really," he said. "See this?" He pointed to another X-ray.

The spot was larger.

"That's how much it's grown in just a week."

I kept looking back and forth between the first X-ray he'd shown me and the second one.

I swallowed. "Can you operate? Get it out?"

He paused a long time.

"We could," he said slowly. "But it's a high-risk procedure. Even if we got it all — and there's no guarantee that we would — she might forget who she is, who you are... most of what's happened in her life so far. She'd have to start all over again."

That was still better than losing her, I told myself. Maybe starting from scratch wouldn't be such a bad idea. We'd always had that connection. Maybe this would even help. Maybe she'd stop hearing her mother's voice and stop feeling guilty about her death.

"You told her this, right, Doc?" I said. "She should be the one to decide."

He frowned. "I tried, but she'd forgotten why she'd come in to see me. She couldn't even remember my name. I'm afraid she's not fit to make medical decisions. You've got her medical power of attorney; it says so on your admission records."

I nodded numbly.

"So, what do you want to do? We'll have to see whether your insurance will cover it, and for how much if..."

"Operate," I said.

There was no hesitation.

"Operate," I repeated.

He nodded. "We can schedule her for next week. We'll have her admitted to the hospital the day before. I'll set it up."

His voice sounded somber. Not encouraging.

I asked him if there was anything I could do in the meantime.

"Are you a religious man?" he asked.

I told him I wasn't.

"Might not be a bad idea to pray anyway."

Tremors

The doctor's appointment had been Friday, and Dr. Thiessen had Molly set to be admitted first thing Monday at City of Hope.

The weekend seemed eternal.

Molly's memory just kept getting worse, and the episodes did, too.

When Monday came, she fought me about going to the hospital, because she was convinced we were headed to the airport and I was going to just leave her there. Or make her get on a plane that was going to crash. "I'm not just a poodle who keeps pissing on the floor that you can take to the pound and get rid of me." It didn't even sound like her. She never talked like that.

"I wouldn't do that," I said.

"How do I know?" she said. "I don't even know who you are. Who are you, anyway? Did Mom and Dad send you..."

"Mom!" she said suddenly.

"Your mom?"

"Yes, she needs my help. Where is she?"

"Your mom's dead."

"No, she's not. You sick liar. Who *are* you, anyway?" she said again.

Freya came and jumped into her lap and started kneading on her, but Molly threw her halfway across the room.

"Get your filthy animal away from me!" she shouted. "Who likes cats, anyway?"

"You do," I said. "Freya's your..."

But her face just went blank then. That crazed-empty look was just empty, and she didn't say a single word after that.

She didn't fight me when I took her to the car, but she didn't do anything else, either. She just walked slowly, like a zombie. The only sounds she made weren't words; they were little moans and sighs that didn't seem to mean anything.

They were short and kind of high-pitched. Like "unh" and "mhnnn" and "ummum."

It was like she wanted to say something, but didn't have the energy, or like she was across some canyon, trying to call to me, but all I could hear was the faintest of sounds.

"It's going to be all right," I kept saying as I drove, but I had no idea if that was true. I was trying to reassure myself as much as her. Maybe more. I told myself she heard me, because she would make those little moans and sighs when I said something.

She sat there next to me, huddled with her knees pulled up against her chest (she hadn't let me put a seatbelt on her). Her big quilt was pulled up around her shoulders — the one her grandmother had made for her, with the purple roses, bees, and sunflowers. It was a heavy quilt, but she was shivering underneath it.

It couldn't be because she's cold, I thought. She seemed almost feverish.

I put my hand on her forehead, but she didn't seem warm. If anything, her skin felt cooler than normal.

She was shaking because she was scared.

Did really think I was going to take her to the airport and just leave her there? Or did she know how awful things were? Did she know about the cancer in her head and how bad the odds were stacked against her?

"What are her chances of making it through?" I'd asked Dr. Thiessen.

He didn't know. Maybe 50-50.

"How much of her life will she remember?"

"If we're lucky, most of it. But I don't want to get your hopes up. We'll have to be very lucky. Chances are, she won't remember much at all."

I wanted to tell him I was paying for him — the best brain surgeon on the West Coast — to be *good*, not lucky. Because insurance wouldn't cover the whole operation, I would be paying. A lot. I didn't care about that. I could worry about how to come up with the money later. But if I was paying him, he'd damn well better do what I was paying to do.

Save Molly. *My* Molly. Not some shadow of a person she used to be.

"What about the cancer? Will it come back?"

"I don't know. No one does in cases like these. It's always a possibility. Sometimes it does, yes."

"What then?"

"We'll have to see."

Molly was still shivering and making those little noises every few minutes, but she had a faraway look in her eyes. I knew now those noises weren't reactions to me or anything I was saying. It was almost like I wasn't even there. Like she was responding to someone else.

But there was no one else here.

"Unh," she whimpered. "Ummum." It almost sounded like...

"...ummom... momma..."

Her mother?

Was she still feeling guilty about that, even now? She couldn't remember who Freya was, who I was, but she could still hear her mother's ghost trying to guilt-trip her about a plane crash years ago she'd had no control over?

Was that all that was left of her... that was going to be left of her... after this was all over? The smartest woman I'd ever met reduced to a vegetable because of, what? A ghost? I didn't believe in ghosts.

I tried to keep my voice level, reassuring. I don't know whether I did or not, though.

"You're mom's not here, Moll. She's at rest now. You don't have to worry about her anymore."

I thought she must have heard me, because she started shaking her head vigorously back and forth. But then I saw it was something else.

Tremors. A seizure. That god damn tumor was giving her a seizure!

We were on the freeway now, and for once, there wasn't much traffic.

I sped up: 75... 80... 90...

I weaved in and out of traffic as I passed cars, one by one. The hospital was maybe five minutes away. I had to get her there so they could do something — anything — to make her better. She was shaking so hard now that the passenger door, which she was leaning against, was shaking, too.

I reached over and locked it, looking away from the road for just a few seconds.

Traffic.

Ahead.

Stopped.

I slammed on the brakes and felt my car swerve to the left, toward the center of the freeway. A concrete barrier.

I didn't have time to stop.

Molly was still shaking. She didn't even seem to know what was happening. She was off somewhere else; where, I didn't know. And I didn't have time to think about it. All I had time to do was direct my car toward the narrow strip of asphalt protected by a wooden "road closed" barrier — maybe three-quarters of a lane between the car-pool lane and that center divider.

I was driving a compact car, a Mini Cooper, thank God. Maybe I could make it.

Maybe...

I winced as we just missed the wooden barrier on one side and a Honda Accord on the other. I *knew* we were going to hit that barrier, but somehow...

We didn't.

I squeezed my shoulders together, as though that would help, and tried to ease onto the brake as the three-quarters-of-a-lane narrowed further in front of me to almost nothing.

Just before it disappeared, we stopped.

I looked over. Molly had stopped shaking. At first, I dared to hope that all the craziness had brought her back to her senses — had jarred her loose from wherever she'd been stuck inside her mind.

But she was just sat there, staring straight ahead, like nothing had happened. She looked numb.

Oh, God. Was she breathing?

I felt her pulse. It was there, calm and steady. I breathed a sigh of relief.

But how could anyone be calm after that?

She blinked every few seconds, but otherwise, she didn't move. She wasn't even making those noises anymore.

I threw off my seatbelt and jumped outside of the car and started screaming, right there on the freeway.

"My wife is dying! I need to get her to the hospital!"

Help me!

STEPHEN H. PROVOST

This...

STEPHEN H. PROVOST

just can't...

STEPHEN H. PROVOST

be...

happening.

STEPHEN H. PROVOST

Vacant

Have you ever had one of those days when everything goes right? Or when everything goes wrong?

Usually, it's one or the other, right?

Everything works or Murphy's Law.

This day was both. Somehow, miraculously, we hadn't been killed in a crash on the Foothill Freeway. Almost as miraculously, a cop had showed up just after I'd started yelling like a madman, had put us both in the car and had taken us to City of Hope.

But none of that meant Molly was any better. She was worse — not shaking, just withdrawn. Not present. Vacant.

Before, it had seemed like she was yelling at me across a canyon. Not it was like she'd given up, turned around, and walked away.

I had to get across that canyon and find her. Somehow.

"Why is she like this?" I asked the nurse when he finally came into Molly's room.

She'd been put there to wait for the operation, which wouldn't be until tomorrow. She was still just staring absently in front of her. If you tried to give her some water to drink, she'd ignore it. If you put a straw in her mouth, she wouldn't suck on it. If you tried to feed her some pudding, she wouldn't swallow. It would come dribbling out of her mouth and roll down her chin.

"What's wrong with her?"

It was a stupid question. I knew it was the tumor. I had expected it would be difficult, but I hadn't thought it would be anything like this. She'd been having those headaches since her parents died, so why was everything getting so much worse so fast?

The nurse dabbed at Molly's chin with a napkin and cleaned her up.

"I think you should talk to the doctor," the nurse said. He didn't say it in the way you might expect: like, "I'm not really sure because I'm not the expert, and you always have to talk to the doctor in situations like these."

It was more like, "I know what's wrong with her, but if I tell you, you'll flip out. You won't do that if you hear it from the doctor. And if you do, *he* can deal with it."

I didn't press him.

The nurse left, and I just sat there with Molly, trying to seem supportive and, at the same time, knowing it didn't matter because she wasn't even aware of me.

I had a sinking feeling I'd gotten there too late. My thoughts ran wild. The tumor had exploded or something inside her head and left her a vegetable. Now, nothing they could do for her would save her.

I shook my head, trying to dislodge that thought. I had to keep hope alive, if only just a little bit, so I didn't lose it completely. That's why they called this place City of Hope, right?

After what seemed like hours, the doctor finally arrived.

I stood up and stepped toward him. "Something's wrong," I said. "She's just sitting there. Not eating. Just staring. What's wrong? Please, God, tell me she's not brain dead."

"Sit down, Mr. Hembridge," he said. "Please."

His voice was soothing but a little anxious. I think he thought I might lose it and go off on him. To be honest, if he *was* thinking that, he might have been right. I was at the end of my rope, and I didn't know what I was capable of. I just knew I wasn't capable of helping Molly right now, and it was driving me crazy.

I nodded and sat down.

The doctor stayed standing.

"Your wife's condition is very serious," he was saying. "To be honest, I don't know why she's acting this way. We'll do a brain scan before we take her in for surgery, but whatever's causing this isn't normal."

"You mean it's not the tumor?"

"I didn't say that, Mr. Hembridge."

I hated how he kept using my name. I knew who the hell I was, and so did he. It wasn't like there was someone else in the room who might think he was talking to them...

My shoulders slumped.

Yes, there was. There was Molly. I was already acting like she wasn't even there. Was I, on some level, preparing myself for how it would feel if she didn't make it? Was I trying to cushion the blow? Was I a monster?

I looked back up at the doctor, squeezing the palms of my hands together. I felt like a penitent sinner asking for redemption. But I wasn't Catholic.

"What *are* you saying then?" I asked. "Is it the tumor, or isn't it."

"It probably is," he said. "It's just that we haven't seen this reaction in someone with this kind of tumor before — at least, not suddenly, like this. But unless she has some underlying condition you haven't told us about..."

I was on a hair-trigger now, and that set me off.

"Something *I* haven't told you about? Like this is all my fault?"

"I didn't say that Mr. Hembridge. Just something that you might have overlooked. Or not known about. Your wife isn't epileptic, is she? Does she have diabetes? Is it possible her blood sugar has crashed and that's what this is?"

"You mean like a diabetic coma?"

"If you want to use that term, then yes."

"I didn't know there was another term for it, but *you're* the doctor," I spat.

I glanced over at Molly. When I lost my

temper like that with other people, she'd give me this disapproving look that brought me back down from it. I'd always hated that. But now, I was hoping against hope to see it.

I didn't.

Her face was still vacant. Expressionless.

"I understand, Mr. Hembridge. I want to know what's causing this, too. If you think of any condition that might be contributing to it, please, just let me know."

He went over and checked her pulse, her heartbeat, her temperature, her breathing, her vital signs.

"Everything seems normal," he said.

The nurse had already done all that and had said the same thing just a few minutes ago. Still, it was a relief.

"Since she's not eating or drinking, I'll order an IV to keep her hydrated. We'll run that brain scan before surgery tomorrow, and I'll leave you alone with her. I'm sure, on some level, she knows you're here."

I knew he was just saying that, trying to be reassuring. I didn't know that at all, and I was her goddamn husband.

I took a deep breath, bit my lip, and forced myself to say "thank you."

"The buzzer is there by her bed, Mr. Hembridge. Call the nurse if there's anything you need."

I nodded.

I leaned back in the uncomfortable wooden visitor's chair and closed my eyes.

Voice

"Allen, are you there? Alley-Oops?"

It was Molly. She was talking to me.

I opened my eyes. I had dozed off. I must have been dreaming, because when I looked at her, she still had that same blank expression on her face.

"Allen?"

I blinked.

Her mouth hadn't moved

"Moll?"

"Yeah, it's me."

I stared at her face, making *sure* her mouth hadn't moved — wouldn't move the next time she spoke.

"Stop staring at her," the voice said. "That's not me."

Her mouth *hadn't* moved.

I was still dreaming. I had to be.

But then the nurse — a short, older woman with slightly hunched shoulders who had relieved the guy who'd been on duty before — came into the room for her hourly check, and all my senses told me I was wide awake.

"Don't worry about her," Molly's voice said. "Listen to me."

I didn't know who she meant by "her." Did she mean Molly, or the person I thought was Molly, staring blankly out into space from the hospital bed? Or did she mean the nurse, who didn't react at all to the voice.

"She can't hear you?" I said.

The nurse turned toward me. "Who can't hear me?" she said. "I didn't say anything."

"No," I said, "I meant my wife can't hear you." I didn't really know what I meant. Obviously, I was hearing voices — or, rather, *a* voice, Molly's voice, in my head. Maybe I had a brain tumor, too. No, of course that wasn't it. I was just going nuts from all the stress.

"Tumors aren't contagious, silly." It was Molly's voice again. How had she known what I was thinking?

"I don't know whether she can hear me or not," the nurse said. "I'm sorry."

"It doesn't matter," I said.

"Of course, she can't hear me," Molly's voice said. "I'm talking to you, inside your head."

That was comforting.

Not.

"From inside *your* head? Like telepathy?" I asked.

"Hmmm?" the nurse said.

"Nothing," I said. I wished she would just go away, and, thankfully, a moment later, she did.

"Not from inside my head," Molly said. "I'm not in there. At least most of me isn't. Most of me is over here."

"Over where?" I asked. The image of her trying to talk to me from across a canyon came back to me, but that had just been my imagination. Hearing her voice was probably just my imagination now, I thought.

But I'd play along. I had nothing better to do except to believe she wasn't talking to me. That she couldn't talk to me. That she had brain cancer that would probably kill her.

I didn't want to think about that, so I kept talking to the voice in my head.

"If you're not inside your head, then where are you?" I asked.

"You don't have to talk out loud," she said. "I can hear your thoughts just fine."

"But where *are* you!" I said, this time in my head, without using my mouth.

"No need to shout," she said.

I really *was* losing it. I'd gone 'round the bend.

"I'm, well... I'm here," she continued. "Do you want to visit me?"

"Visit you? What do you mean?"

"I mean come and see me, silly. Oh, guess what! I found Mom."

"You found your mom?"

"Will you please just stop repeating everything I say. You know how annoying that is."

I did. She'd told me more times than I could count.

"Okay," I said. "How do I 'visit you'?"

"Close your eyes and relax and think of me, and you'll find your way. Just follow the sound of my voice."

I closed my eyes, then opened them again.

I *couldn't* relax.

How could she have found her mother? Her mother was dead. My heart started beating faster. None of this was real.

I stared at Molly, lying there in bed, her eyes open, blinking every so often, but seeming entirely unaware of anything. Then, as I watched, her eyes slowly closed. Was she going to sleep? Maybe this meant something! If she could go to sleep, it meant some part of her was still here with me.

It meant there was hope.

But what if she didn't wake up?

The voice came again. "Yes, some part of me is still there. But not very much. Most of me is here. Please trust me, Allen-a-Dale. Close your eyes. Relax. And follow my voice."

"But..."

"I know this doesn't make sense to you. It didn't make sense to you that I knew you had that ring in your pocket before you proposed. Or that I knew Atlantis was real. And it is! Or that I knew Mom had been calling out to me for help, because she was. But it's all okay now. I found her, and she forgave me, and everything's okay. The guilt is gone and everything. It's all better now."

I took one more look at Molly lying there in bed and closed my eyes.

"Just trust me," she said. "Always trust me."

Tunnel

Everything was dark at first.

"This way, Alley-Oops. Over here. That's right."

I could hear the sound of her voice getting louder, even though there wasn't an actual sound, so I couldn't actually "hear" it.

I put both hands out in front of me, groping like I was walking blindfolded in a game of pin-the-tail-on-the-donkey. I felt something before I saw anything. I felt her hands, taking mine, holding them.

"Oh, thank God," she said. "I missed you so much."

I opened my eyes — I didn't realize I'd had them closed — and there she was, smiling at me like she had been when we'd first met. She looked the same. Her face was full of life and calm. Not anxious or, worse, vacant, the way it had been in the hospital room.

"Where are we?" I said.

"We're here," she said. "Look around you."

I did, but I wasn't really sure what I was seeing. It was all blurred and hazy, shimmering like heat on an asphalt road in summer. It made me feel slightly queasy.

I looked back at her, and everything about her was crystal clear. As clear as it ever had been, if not clearer.

I shook my head. "What's happened?" I said.

"Oh," she said, a little of the joy leaving her face. "I didn't realize. Mom says that when you don't belong here, you can't see everything the way we can. I can't even see it as well as *she* can yet, but I'll be able to, soon. She tells me I will, and I believe her."

"What do you mean I don't belong here? I belong with you. That's what we always said."

She looked a little sad. "I know, Alley-Oops, but not now. You can only stay here for a little while."

Then it hit me like a brick.

She'd found her mom. Her mom was dead. That meant *she* was...

I couldn't bring myself to say the last word, not even just in my mind.

Instead I said, "You said your mom was here, but I can't see her. Where is she?"

"You can't see her because you don't belong here," Molly said. "I can see her because I do. Now. I'm sorry."

"You *don't* belong here!" I said. "You belong back at home with me."

She shook her head sadly.

"You're *not* dead!" I protested. "I saw you back there in the hospital. The doctor said your chances were 50-50, and he's the best neurosurgeon on the West Coast. He'll save you and you'll be all back to normal in no time. Then we can go home and you can see Freya again, and everything will be back to normal."

"Tell Freya I didn't mean it when I threw her off my lap like that," Molly said. "I wasn't myself. Things like that happen when you're in transition. I'm really so sorry about everything I said to you about the airport. Can you ever forgive me? Please say you'll forgive me."

"Of course, I forgive you." I reached out and touched her cheek, and it shimmered like everything else around me. I wasn't even sure I felt anything when my fingers touched her.

"You've been going through hell," I said. "There's nothing to forgive."

Then my mind grasped onto one of the other words she'd used.

Transition.

"You're not dead," I repeated.

That queasy feeling was getting worse. I didn't know if it was because the thought of Molly dying made me feel that way, or whether it was from the vertigo this place seemed to be causing — whatever this place was.

"Death isn't the way you think it is," she said. It was her old, philosophical, sharp-as-hell self talking, explaining something to me I didn't understand.

Part of me was relieved that she'd found that part of herself again. Another part of me was scared.

Scared to death.

I heard a voice then from somewhere very far away. I recognized it. It was Dr. Thiessen, saying something to the nurse. It seemed like it was coming through an echo chamber.

"Let him sleep," he told the nurse. "He'll need all the strength he can get." Then something unintelligible, followed by "... at death's doorstep." More words I couldn't make out, and "...can make it long enough for us to do the surgery..." His voice trailed off.

Molly laughed.

It sounded almost surreal, like one of those insane laughs from a villain in a superhero movie. Except it wasn't insane. Molly genuinely seemed to have thought it was funny.

"You heard that?" I said.

"No. I heard you thinking about what you heard, though. And he's got it all wrong. There's no doorstep to death, because death isn't a door, it's more like a tunnel."

"A tunnel?"

"Mm-hmm. At least it is for some of us. If you're hit by a car or have a massive heart attack and go out all at once, it's more like a door, but for me, it's more like a tunnel."

I was about to tell her I wasn't going to let her die, but she kept going before I could say it.

"Remember how your grandfather lost a little bit of himself every week? He became harder and harder to reach, like part of him was just... leaving, and there was less and less of him still there with you? Like just his body, but not much else?"

I nodded. I'd used those very words to tell her what it had felt like. It felt the same way with her now, but a lot worse. I'd never been that close to my grandfather, but I'd never been closer to *anyone* than I was to Molly.

"Did you ever wonder where the rest of him went?" she asked.

I never had. It had never occurred to me that it had gone *anywhere*. I just assumed it had been lost altogether.

"When your grandfather started showing signs of Alzheimer's, it was like he was entering a tunnel, and a part of him came out the other side and ended up here, but a part of him was still there, with you. It's like being stretched, you know? Like a rubber band or silly putty — stretched so far that part of you is at one end of the tunnel, and part of you's at the other. It's very painful and disorienting.

"Remember when I heard Mom crying out, 'Help me!' as she was dying? That was when she was trapped underwater and couldn't breathe. She was starting to lose consciousness and was caught between your world and this one. There's no place scarier. She was terrified."

"What about all those other times you said you heard her?"

"They were echoes," Molly said. "Echoes of my own guilty conscience."

At least I had been right about that much. It *had* all been in her head. Now it probably was, too. More likely, it was all in my head. I was so stressed, so frightened, that I'd turned my worst fears into this nightmare. But then I looked at Molly again, and she was no nightmare. The person with the vacant stare in the hospital bed was the nightmare; the woman here in front of me was my dream come true. Just like she'd always been.

None of this made sense.

What was she trying to say? People aren't like silly putty. They can't be stretched through some imaginary tunnel like rubber bands. I was the physicist. I knew better. This was madness.

Or was it?

I stopped myself.

In quantum physics, there's this idea that things can be in two places at once. It's more complicated than that, but that's the gist of it. Was she saying that people could occupy more than one place at the same time? Not the people themselves, but their souls, their minds, their essence — whatever you wanted to call it. Whatever it was that makes us who we are.

"Not quite," she said. She must have heard me thinking again. "But it's kind of like that, yes. If you need an analogy to wrap your science-crazy brain around, that works as well as any."

The queasiness was becoming nausea. I felt like I was doubling over, getting ready to puke.

"You can't stay here much longer," she said. "It will tear you apart, because you don't belong here. I just wanted to see you one last time, because it will be a while before you come through here. Then we can be together again."

I tried to force the contents of my stomach back down again, even though I was vaguely aware that it was just a feeling and that my stomach wasn't really here — wherever "here" was.

"This is all an illusion," I said firmly. "I'm dreaming."

"Do you really want this to be just a dream?" Molly said. She looked stricken. "Didn't you want to see me this last time?"

Everything was spinning now. I fumbled for words.

"Of course, I..."

She grabbed me and pulled me close and kissed me.

"You have to go back now. There's no more time," she said.

And I said, "Then, you're coming with me."

I've got to...

STEPHEN H. PROVOST

retrace...

STEPHEN H. PROVOST

my...

STEPHEN H. PROVOST

steps.

STEPHEN H. PROVOST

Back

She tried to pull loose from my grip, but I wouldn't let go of her hand.

"I can't," she said. "Please, Allen, you have to let me go."

But I wouldn't. If this tunnel of hers had brought her here, I could use it to bring her back. It was simple logic. If A=B, then B=A. Reverse the flow.

"Allen, it doesn't work that way. It's not like an electrical current; it's like a river. You can't turn it around. You have to let me go. For your sake. I can't go back there, but you have to. Without me.

If you try to take me with you, we'll both end up..."

"End up how? And how do you know it doesn't work?" I was yelling in my thoughts. "Have you ever *tried* it?"

"No," she said. She was crying now. Please, just let me go. I know it doesn't work because death's a one-way tunnel. *No one* ever comes back from it."

"BUT YOU'RE NOT DEAD YET!" I shouted.

"I will be soon. Most of me already is. You can't reverse it."

"How do you know? I've heard people say they've seen a white light and stopped breathing and their heart has stopped and they've been pronounced dead and they still come back. That means you can, too."

"It's not like that." She was pleading now. "I know."

"You *can't* know. It *can't* be true." I was starting to cry now, too. And I wouldn't let go of her hand, no matter how hard she pulled at me; no matter how much she tried to claw my fingers off. They weren't really fingers. They were just expressions of my soul's desperation. And because I was more desperate than she was, she couldn't break free.

I convinced myself it was because a part of her was still back there, lying in that hospital room, clinging to life, *wanting* to live. Wanting to come home with me. Wanting for that one-in-a million recovery to be true.

Maybe it was that, or maybe I had just become so disoriented I'd started to go crazy.

"You have to go!" she was wailing. "PLEASE!"

"Not without YOU!"

I held her hand fast and started pulling her. I don't know how I knew the way. Probably, I just wanted to get away from the hazy, swirling, nauseating place I'd been in and go in the opposite direction.

"Please! Allen! JUST TRUST ME."

There were those words again. But I couldn't trust her now, any more than I'd trusted her before about Atlantis or any of the other weird things we told me.

"You have to let go," she was saying. "If you love me, YOU HAVE TO LET GO!"

"Can't you see I'm doing this *because* I love you?"

"But you don't understand. That's not the way out. If you try to take me with you, you'll wind up... please, Allen, you don't want to go there. I don't want you to go there. You'll destroy us both."

Destroy us? What was the worst that could happen? We'd both wind up dead and just end up right back here again? I supposed that wouldn't be so bad. At least then I'd "belong there" and wouldn't be nauseated all the time. In theory. If this wasn't just a bad dream. Which it probably was, but if it wasn't, I couldn't just leave Molly behind.

I couldn't. Not again.

I remembered what had happened when I went off to work on that project in Stockholm all those years ago. If I hadn't gone back, it would have been the biggest mistake of my life.

Molly was just forty-five now, and I was only forty-three. We had half our lives left to look forward to together — not in some surreal ghost land at the other end of some warped tunnel, but a real life in a real house with a real cat and real food and real intimacy and real ... everything.

"Allen, NO! We can't go back that way!" She was screaming now. "It's a dead end."

But I didn't listen. I didn't let go.

I couldn't.

I wish I had.

"It's now or never," I said. "Let's go."

STEPHEN H. PROVOST

Now

I open my eyes and try to look around. I can't see Molly, can't feel her hand. But didn't let go. I'm sure I didn't.

It's not just Molly that I can't see. I can't see anything.

I hear voices, but none of them are hers.

"Is she prepped for surgery?"

"Yes, doctor."

"Okay, let's get started stat. I'm afraid we're about to lose this patient."

It sounds like I'm in the operating room, but that can't be. I'm asleep in that uncomfortable wooden chair, sitting across from Molly. I have to be. I had this awful dream and... Why can't I open my eyes?

I reach up and try to pry them open with my fingers, but I can't even *feel* my fingers on my eyelids.

I'm still dreaming.

I must be.

And I'm hearing those voices because I'm about to wake up.

"Come on, Allen. Wake up. GOD DAMN IT! WAKE THE HELL UP!"

"Blood pressure is steady. Are you ready to begin?"

"It's now or never. Let's go."

Then I realize where I am, and what Molly meant when she said I couldn't take her back with me that way. I'm not inside my mind anymore; I'm inside *hers* — or the dying part of hers that was lying on that hospital bed and must now be in surgery on the table in the operating room at City of Hope.

I don't know how I got here, but it must have been because I tried to take her back with me, instead of just coming back alone.

But if I'm here, where's Molly? Shouldn't she be here, too?

It occurs to me, in a flash of understanding, why she hadn't wanted to come back. She hadn't wanted to get stuck inside a shell of a body again.

"I'm sorry!" I yell. "Where are you?"

No answer.

She must be here with me. I have to find her. But I can't see anything. Can't hear anything. Can barely move. It's like being buried alive in that coffin, only now I can feel the walls of the coffin closing in around me, all the air being sucked out. I'm gasping, like in that dream with the birthday candles.

I feel utterly alone.

Except Molly's here with me. She has to be. Where...?

I feel nauseated again, but I shouldn't feel that way. I'm back from the dead, or wherever I'd been that she said I didn't belong, that place where I'd felt nauseated before. Maybe I'm just feeling what Molly's feeling, now that I'm inside her brain.

The brain with the tumor.

The brain that, Dr. Thiessen had said, might not be able to remember anything once the operation was over.

No. That can't be.

It's all a dream.

I'm not really hearing the voices I think I'm hearing.

"Ready for incision."

"Pressure."

"Scalpel."

I scream in anguish as I feel something slicing into my skull.

"STOP!"

Oh, God. What's happening?

Help me!

But no one answers. I feel the pain, and then, a flash of light. Or something like light. I know I can't really see it, because my eyes are closed, but it's just as real, just as bright, and just as sudden.

Blinding.

And darkness again.

I wait.

Minutes pass, or maybe hours. I'm not sure. Then the voices return.

"We got part of it, but we couldn't get it all."

"That's all we could do."

"If we'd done any more, we would have killed him."

Him?

"He'll die anyway, or be a vegetable. He'll be on life support."

"I know."

"What are you going to tell his girlfriend? She seems so scared."

"I've never seen anyone so in love with someone. I mean, she hasn't slept in days. She came all the way over from L.A. here to Stockholm just to be here with him, even though he doesn't know she's here."

"Maybe he does know, on some level."

Did that person say Stockholm? I'm not in Stockholm. And I don't have a girlfriend. I have a wife. I'm married. I'm happily married...

"We just tell her the truth. We couldn't get all of the tumor. He's been in this coma since he collapsed in Dr. Larsson's office two weeks ago, and when it's been this long, they hardly ever come out of it."

"There's still a chance, though."

"Even if he does, he won't remember much. We had to take a good chunk of his memory center."

"And we still didn't get it all."

"Okay, no use kicking ourselves over it."

"I'll never get used to this sort of thing — leaving someone in limbo between life and death like that. It's like they're stuck in a tunnel that's blocked from both sides."

"That's one way to look at it."

"Scary."

"Yeah."

The nausea is coming in waves now. I can't think. I can't form words. I see bees buzzing in a field of spring blossoms, flying from a garden of purple roses to a sea of sunflowers. A scene from a childhood picnic. Or Molly's quilt. Which one? It doesn't make sense.

And now it's slipping away. Being stripped from my mind like someone's peeled back a roll of tape and pulled it away. What was it?

I'm trying to remember my life with her.

I hear her voice in the distance: "I'm here. I'm here. I won't leave you." Someone holding my hand...

What's her name again? I just had it, but now it's gone. Polly... no... Holly... That's not right either. I can't remember! But we were so happy. For twenty years. Or maybe it was fifteen. How long has it been?

Were those years all just in my head? Not her head... but mine? No cat... or was it a dog? No tunnel to that other place?

Did none of that ever really happen?

None of... what?

I'm trying to remember. I can't.

My head hurts. Like a migraine.

I started working on a project in Stockholm, but then...? What then? There was a woman... Or was there? I'm not sure now.

I'm not sure of anything.

It's all just fading away, and I'm not sure if it was ever really there to begin with. I feel like I felt when I was a little kid, when my parents told me about airplanes that crashed in the Bermuda Triangle, and they said Atlantis was there, under the sea, too...

Or did they?

I thought I remembered those stories.

For a minute.

What stories?

What are stories?

Somebody. Please...

Help me!

Love never dies
a natural death.

Anais Nin

STEPHEN H. PROVOST

Fin

STEPHEN H. PROVOST

About the author

During a 30-year career in journalism, Stephen H. Provost worked as a managing editor, copy desk chief, columnist and reporter at five newspapers. Now a full-time author, he has written on such diverse topics as American highways, dragons, mutant superheroes, mythic archetypes, language, department stores and his hometown. Read his blogs and keep up with his activities at stephenhprovost.com.

Also by the author

Works of Fiction
  Nightmare's Eve
  Memortality (The Memortality Saga, Vol. 1)
  Paralucidity (The Memortality Saga, Vol. 2)
  The Talismans of Time
    (Academy of the Lost Labyrinth, Vol. 1)
  Pathfinder of Destiny
    (Academy of the Lost Labyrinth, Vol. 2)
  The Only Dragon
  Identity Break
  Feathercap

Works of Nonfiction
  Yesterday's Highways
    (America's Historic Highways, Vol. 1)
  America's First Highways
    (America's Historic Highways, Vol. 2)
  Highway 99 (California's Historic Highways, Vol. 1)
  Highway 101 (California's Historic Highways, Vol. 2)
  A Whole Different League
  The Legend of Molly Bolin
  Fresno Growing Up
  Martinsville Memories
  50 Undefeated

DEATH'S DOORSTEP

The Osiris Testament
   (The Phoenix Chronicles, Vol. 1)
The Way of the Phoenix
   (The Phoenix Chronicles, Vol. 2)
The Gospel of the Phoenix
   (The Phoenix Chronicles, Vol. 3)
Forged in Ancient Fires
   (The Phoenix Principle, Vol. 1)
Messiah in the Making
   (The Phoenix Principle, Vol. 2)
Please Stop Saying That!
Political Psychosis
Media Meltdown in the Age of Trump
Requiem for a Phantom God

Praise for other works

"The genres in this volume span horror, fantasy, and science-fiction, and each is handled deftly. ... **Nightmare's Eve** should be on your reading list. The stories are at the intersection of nightmare and lucid dreaming, up ahead a signpost ... next stop, your reading pile. Keep the nightlight on."

— R.B. Payne, Cemetery Dance

"The complex idea of mixing morality and mortality is a fresh twist on the human condition. ... **Memortality** is one of those books that will incite more questions than it answers. And for fandom, that's a good thing."

— Ricky L. Brown, Amazing Stories

"Punchy and fast paced, **Memortality** reads like a graphic novel. ... (Provost's) style makes the trippy landscapes and mind-bending plot points more believable and adds a thrilling edge to this vivid crossover fantasy."

— Foreword Reviews

"**Memortality** by Stephen Provost is a highly original, thrilling novel unlike anything else out there."

> — David McAfee, bestselling author of
> 33 A.D., 61 A.D., and 79 A.D.

"Profusely illustrated throughout, **Highway 99** is unreservedly recommended as an essential and core addition to every community and academic library's California History collections."

> — California Bookwatch

"As informed and informative as it is entertaining and absorbing, **Fresno Growing Up** is very highly recommended for personal, community, and academic library 20th Century American History collections."

> — John Burroughs, Reviewer's Bookwatch

"Provost sticks mostly to the classics: vampires, ghosts, aliens, and even dragons. But trekking familiar terrain allows the author to subvert readers' expectations. ... Provost's poetry skillfully displays the same somber themes as the stories. ...

Worthy tales that prove external forces are no more terrifying than what's inside people's heads."

— Kirkus Reviews on **Nightmare's Eve**

"… an engaging narrative that pulls the reader into the story and onto the road. … I highly recommend **Highway 99: The History of California's Main Street**, whether you're a roadside archaeology nut or just someone who enjoys a ripping story peppered with vintage photographs."

— Barbara Gossett,
Society for Commercial Archaeology Journal